Good Night, D.W.

by Marc Brown

LITTLE, BROWN AND COMPANY

New York ∿ An AOL Time Warner Company

It was time for bed.
Dad tucked in D.W. and gave her a kiss. Mom turned on the nightlight.
She gave D.W. a kiss, too.
"Good night, D.W.!" they said together.

D.W. tried to fall asleep. But she couldn't. She was wide awake. "Is anybody out there?" she called.

Arthur came in. "What's the matter?" he asked.
"I can't sleep," said D.W.
"When I can't sleep, I think about one of the Bionic Bunny's adventures," said Arthur. "That always tires me out."

"I bet the Bionic Bunny has trouble falling asleep," said D.W.
"He must have a lot on his mind, too."
Arthur rolled his eyes. "Good night, D.W.!" he said.
"I've got homework to do."

"Is anybody out there?" D.W. called again.
Dad came in. "What's the matter?" he asked.

"I can't sleep," said D.W.
"Try counting sheep," said Dad. "Nice, fluffy sheep jumping over a fence."

"Did you ever wonder about sheep?" said D.W. "When do they sleep? They must not have time if they're so busy jumping over fences."

Dad sighed. "Good night, D.W.!" he said. "See you in the morning."

"Is anybody out there?" D.W. called a third time.
Mom came in. "What's the matter?" she asked.
"I can't sleep," said D.W.
"Just relax," said Mom. "Think about happy things . . . like
going to the beach."

"But whenever I go to the beach, my bathing suit gets full of sand. I could never sleep thinking about all that itchy sand on me."

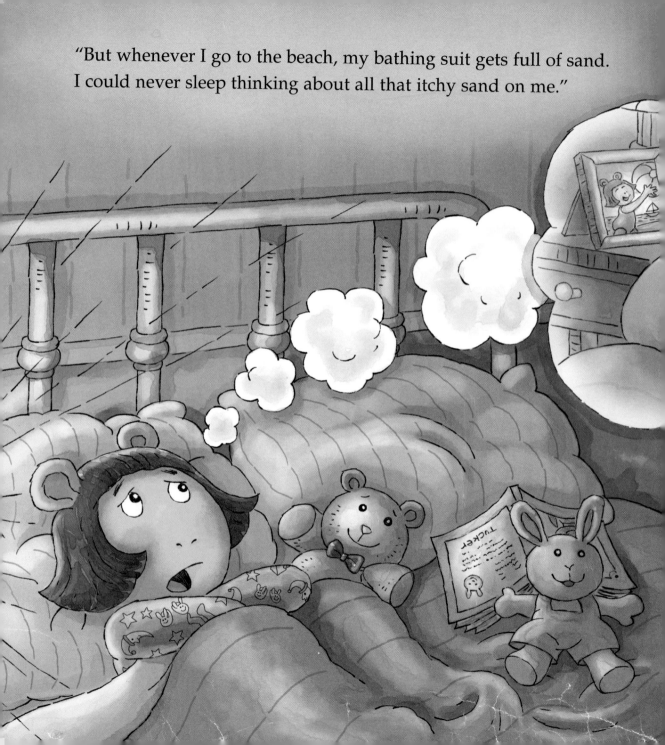

Her mother shook her head. "Good night, D.W.!"
she said. "Close your eyes."

D.W. closed her eyes. She tried thinking about the Bionic Bunny.

And the beach.

And fluffy white sheep.

But of course, none of it worked.

This time everyone rushed in together.
"What is it now?" asked Dad.

"How do you expect me to sleep?" said D.W. "The wind is blowing.
And the bed is creaking. And Kate is making weird sounds!"
D.W. stopped to blink a few times.

"Besides, a tree could fall on the house. And there could be
a monster under the bed. Or in the closet. Or both!"
D.W. yawned a giant yawn.

"There are a gazillion reasons why I can't fall asleep," said D.W., closing her eyes. "I could go on . . . and on . . . and on . . ." And she did.

But only in her dreams.

Good night, D.W.!